The Architect and the Magistrate

JUSTIN CLARK

Copyright © 2024 Justin Clark.

All rights reserved. No part of this book may be reproduced, stored, or transmitted by any means—whether auditory, graphic, mechanical, or electronic—without written permission of both publisher and author, except in the case of brief excerpts used in critical articles and reviews. Unauthorized reproduction of any part of this work is illegal and is punishable by law.

ISBN: 979-8-89031-886-2 (sc)
ISBN: 979-8-89031-887-9 (hc)
ISBN: 979-8-88640-037-3 (e)

Because of the dynamic nature of the Internet, any web addresses or links contained in this book may have changed since publication and may no longer be valid. The views expressed in this work are solely those of the author and do not necessarily reflect the views of the publisher, and the publisher hereby disclaims any responsibility for them.

One Galleria Blvd., Suite 1900, Metairie, LA 70001
(504) 702-6708

The Architect and the Magistrate

One morning a boy named Cody McCoy left his farmhouse in Kentucky to go to his favorite spot on his family's land. The place that the boy seeks is a small meadow at the end of a narrow trail through the woods. The meadow opens up wide just after the trail and is full of high yellow and green grasses almost too tall for the boy to see over. The grasses always seem to dance with the familiar wind that passes through the meadow every day.

Cody heard of a legend about a small Magistrate who lives within not only his family's land but lives within all of the earth. He heard that this Magistrate will speak to anyone who takes the time to truly listen to what he has to say. The Magistrate teaches people about all things in life. Cody has been thinking about creating a house in his favorite meadow and thought that maybe if he went there that he could find this mysterious Magistrate who he thought could teach him how to go about building this house.

When Cody got to the meadow, as usual the wind was talking quietly to the yellow and green grasses and they were swaying back and forth to the gentle voice of the wind. Cody thought to himself that it was almost as if the wind was telling the meadow a bedtime story.

Cody sat down in the tall grass and listened to the wind himself as it seemed to calm him. As the wind spoke to him, he began to see much more going on in the meadow that he did not see before. He saw beautiful yellow butterflies soaring just above the wildflowers as if they were gliding on the wind like waves. He thought to himself, wow it is as if they are playing a game with the sky itself. As if they are connected to the wind by strings.

He noticed that there were many bumble bees hovering like mini helicopters just above the petals of the wildflowers in the meadow as if they could stay still in the air all day.

Cody wondered how they could stay there so long as it seemed that they did not use the wind at all.

The bumble bees seemed to be bossing the wind around.

Cody looked next to him and saw a grasshopper clinging to a blade of grass.

The grasshopper's legs looked almost like the grass he was perched on and if Cody did not pay attention, the grasshopper disappeared. It was as if the grasshopper was part of a magic show for Cody himself as he was disappearing and reappearing.

He was beautiful but only if you pay close attention and could spot him.

Cody felt something shimmering around him so he turned his head in a circle to glance at the entire meadow and noticed that the meadow was wrapped by tall trees. He then looked closer and saw that the leaves on the trees were each being rocked back and forth by the same wind that keeps talking to him. It is as if the wind is telling the leaves the same story as it was telling the tall grasses. It seems that the wind is speaking to all living things in the meadow through it's gentle touch.

Then all of a sudden it came to him. The Magistrate was talking to him through the wind, the butterflies, the grasses, the bumble bees, the grasshoppers, the trees and the leaves. It was telling him to look and listen closely and you will find what you are looking for. The Magistrate was telling him that each of these living things that you were seeing, feeling, and hearing today, can help you with anything that you may need.

He is telling him that each of these creatures has a connection to the meadow and that we must all have a connection to what we live around or we do not live at all. Cody understood now.

The Magistrate had all the time been giving him ideas of how to build his house, showing him many conversations going on between each creature and its surroundings, which for the creature is the meadow. The house could come out of the ground, and soar in the wind above the wild flowers like a butterfly or it could hove over the meadow as if to own the sky like a bumble bee. It could blend into its surrounding like a grasshopper and disappear or reappear at will or it could shimmer in the wind like a leaf.

Although Cody loved all the creatures that he had been shown today and thought that each of them had very special things about them, his favorite creature that he saw today was the beautiful yellow butterfly soaring just above the wildflowers as if it were gliding on the wind like waves. he thought that the butterfly's connection to the meadow was through the sky and that it was magnificent. Their flight was to him an ongoing living story between the earth and the sky. The butterfly's body seemed nore of the earth but the wings were of the sky and it could soar through the wind like no other.

Cody was set on building his house in a way that

brought the earth and the sky together as he believed the butterfly did.

He will build a floor on the earth of which to live on, however the roof will be that of a

butterfly's wing which bring the sky into the house and connect the ground to the sky.

He hopes that his house will be an ongoing living story between the earth and sky as the butterfly's flight is to him.

Cody's House in the Meadow

www.ingramcontent.com/pod-product-compliance
Lightning Source LLC
LaVergne TN
LVHW072131060526
838201LV00071B/5012